Dear Parent:

Congratulations! Your child is taking the first steps on an exciting journey. The destination? Independent reading!

STEP INTO READING® will help your child get there. The program offers five steps to reading success. Each step includes fun stories and colorful art. There are also Step into Reading Sticker Books, Step into Reading Math Readers, Step into Reading Phonics Readers, Step into Reading Write-In Readers, and Step into Reading Phonics Boxed Sets—a complete literacy program with something for every child.

Learning to Read, Step by Step!

Ready to Read   Preschool–Kindergarten
• big type and easy words • rhyme and rhythm • picture clues
For children who know the alphabet and are eager to begin reading.

Reading with Help   Preschool–Grade 1
• basic vocabulary • short sentences • simple stories
For children who recognize familiar words and sound out new words with help.

Reading on Your Own   Grades 1–3
• engaging characters • easy-to-follow plots • popular topics
For children who are ready to read on their own.

Reading Paragraphs   Grades 2–3
• challenging vocabulary • short paragraphs • exciting stories
For newly independent readers who read simple sentences with confidence.

Ready for Chapters   Grades 2–4
• chapters • longer paragraphs • full-color art
For children who want to take the plunge into chapter books but still like colorful pictures.

STEP INTO READING® is designed to give every child a successful reading experience. The grade levels are only guides. Children can progress through the steps at their own speed, developing confidence in their reading, no matter what their grade.

Remember, a lifetime love of reading starts with a single step!

To my buddy Christopher Winskill
—J. W.

Copyright © 2014 Disney Enterprises, Inc. All rights reserved. Published in the United States by Golden Books, an imprint of Random House Children's Books, a division of Random House LLC, a Penguin Random House Company, 1745 Broadway, New York, NY 10019, and in Canada by Random House of Canada Limited, Toronto, in conjunction with Disney Enterprises, Inc. Based on the Mowgli stories in *The Jungle Book* and *The Second Jungle Book* by Rudyard Kipling.

Step into Reading, Random House, and the Random House colophon are registered trademarks of Random House LLC.

Visit us on the Web!
StepIntoReading.com
randomhouse.com/kids

Educators and librarians, for a variety of teaching tools, visit us at RHTeachersLibrarians.com

Library of Congress Cataloging-in-Publication Data
Winskill, John.
Jungle friends / by John Winskill.   p.   cm. — (Step into reading. A step 1 book)
SUMMARY: Easy-to-read text introduces a number of Mowgli's friends from the animated Disney version of The Jungle Book.
ISBN 978-0-7364-2089-1 (trade) — ISBN 978-0-7364-8017-8 (lib. bdg.) —
ISBN 978-0-7364-3201-6 (ebook)
[1. Jungles—Fiction.   2. Animals—Fiction.   3. India—Fiction.]
I. Title.   II. Series: Step into reading. Step 1 book.
PZ7.W729897 Ju   2003b   [E]—dc21   2002151942

Printed in the United States of America   15 14 13 12 11 10

Jungle Friends

By John Winskill

Illustrated by the Disney Global Artists

Random House 🏠 New York

Mowgli lives in
the jungle.
He has lots of friends.

Scaly friends.

Furry friends.

Feathered friends.

Giant friends.

Mowgli has fun with
his jungle friends.

Every day they
march and play.

They run.

They swing.

They eat.

They dance.

But of all his jungle friends . . .

Big Baloo is his favorite.